Green

What colour is
the see-saw?

Tom and Harry are having fun on the
see-saw. Susan holds on tightly to the
roundabout.

Black

What colour is
the camera?

Click! The photographer is taking the
family group. Don't they look handsome?

Brown

Who is in the brown boat?

How many boats are on the lake? Oh dear,
Tom and Harry have bumped into William.
Luckily no one falls into the water.

White

What colour is the cloth?

Tom and Harry are in trouble again.
The cloth is covered with dirty footprints.

Orange

What colour is
Polly's kite?

It is a fine day for flying kites.
What colour is Tom and Harry's ball?

Red

What colour are the bandsmen's coats?

Father and Mother enjoy listening to the band. Tom and Harry are marching round the bandstand.

Pink

What colour
balloon is
William
buying?

It is nice to rest in the shade of a tree.
Father's hat will soon be covered in ice cream.

Yellow

Who is sailing the yellow boat?

Susan has caught a yellow boot in her net.
Do you think there are any fish in the pond?

Blue

What colour is the engine?

Toot, toot, goes the engine. Victoria stays with Mother and Father while the others go for a ride.

It is time to go home for tea. The pink
balloon is tied to the pram. Susan is
carrying her purple flowers. Polly has her

orange kite and William holds his yellow boat.
What a lovely day in the park!